W9-CUB-335

LEGO STAR WARS™

BUILD YOUR OWN
ADVENTURE
GALACTIC MISSIONS

CONTENTS

MEET SEB ASTRO

As a proud member of the Bespin Wing Guard, brave Seb Astro is responsible for keeping law and order on Cloud City. A giant mining station that floats above the planet Bespin, Cloud City attracts all kinds of rogues and wrongdoers—so Seb must be ready for anything! He is an expert pilot, and likes nothing more than a mission that calls for him to fly a cloud car!

LOOKING OUT FOR LANDO

Seb's boss is the Baron Administrator of Cloud City, Lando Calrissian. Lando is a good guy at heart, but he has made lots of enemies over the years. Seb has his work cut out when it comes to protecting Lando and his possessions!

I'M ALWAYS ON DUTY AND READY TO SERVE!

Determined expression

Blaster

Gold-trimmed uniform

CORELLIA

When the Republic fell, an evil Empire took its place. Grim and grimy planets like Corellia represented the Imperial ideal—endless factories churning out warships and a population of tired workers and small-time crooks with little hope for the future. Something had to change!

NABOO

During the Old Republic, most of the galaxy was at peace, and Naboo was a center of art and culture. But in the last days of the Republic, greedy businesses sent droid armies to destroy the peace, hoping to make money from the chaos they caused.

THE PLANETS

The galaxy is a very big place, especially when you're a LEGO® minifigure! In this book, you'll set course for different times and distant places—from peaceful Naboo in the Old Republic to lonely Jakku after the fall of the Empire. But wherever you go, you'll find heroes fighting for freedom and justice, and villains who want to have everything their own way!

SCARIF

As the Empire reached its peak, it extended its reach to the Outer Rim of the galaxy. It built huge security complexes on planets such as Scarif, with no respect for the beautiful surroundings. Yet at the same time, a ragtag Rebel Alliance was forming to challenge the rule of the Emperor.

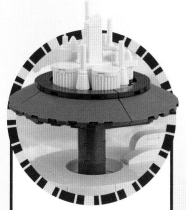

BESPIN

When Galactic Civil War raged between the Empire and the rebels, Cloud City was at peace. Run by Lando Calrissian, the mining complex floated above the planet Bespin without taking a side. When he finally had to choose, Lando realized he was a rebel!

JAKKU

Thanks to heroes from across the galaxy, the Empire was eventually defeated, leaving wrecked ships across the desert world of Jakku. A peaceful New Republic was formed, but the evil First Order rose up to threaten the galaxy once more, and a brave Resistance came together to fight them.

BUILD YOUR OWN ADVENTURE

YOU'LL PICK IT UP IN NO TIME!

In the pages of this book, you will discover an exciting LEGO® Star Wars™ adventure. You will also see some clever ideas for LEGO Star Wars models that might inspire you to create your own. Building LEGO models from your imagination is creative and endlessly fun. There are no limits to what you can build. This is your adventure, so jump right in and start building!

HOW TO USE THIS BOOK

This book will not show you exactly how to build the models, because you may not have the same bricks in your LEGO collection. It will give you lots of ideas and show you useful building tips and model breakdowns that will help you when it comes to building your own models. Here's how the pages work:

Breakdowns of models feature useful build tips

"What will you build?" flashes give you even more ideas for models you could build

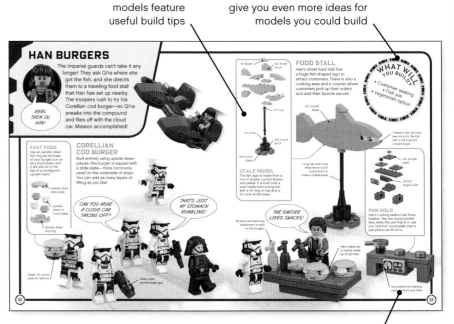

Special features or elements on models are annotated

WHRRRRR!

EYE CAUTION
For models with shooting functions, do not aim the shooter at eyes.

HELLO, I'M ROD GILLIES.

MEET THE BUILDER

Rod Gillies is a LEGO fan and super-builder, and he made the inspirational LEGO models that can be found in this book. To make the models just right for the LEGO *Star Wars* world, Rod worked with the LEGO *Star Wars* team at the LEGO Group headquarters in Billund, Denmark. Use Rod's creations to inspire your own unique models!

BEFORE YOU BEGIN

Here are five handy hints to keep in mind every time you get out your bricks and prepare to build:

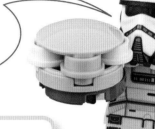

TROOPERS JUST LOVE BURGERS!

ORGANIZE YOUR BRICKS

Organizing bricks into colors and types can save you time when you're building.

MAKE YOUR MODEL STABLE

Make a model that's sturdy enough to play with. You'll find useful tips for making a stable model throughout this book.

BE CREATIVE

If you don't have the perfect piece, find a creative solution! Look for a different piece that can create a similar effect.

THINK LIKE AN ENGINEER

Use real-world engineering principles to help build your model. Should it be slim and speedy, or stable and strong?

HAVE FUN

Don't worry if your model goes wrong. Turn it into something else or start again. The fun is in the building!

BUILDER TALK

Did you know that LEGO® builders have their own language? You will find the terms below used a lot in this book. Here's what they mean:

WITHOUT THESE PARTS, I'M NOTHING!

MEASUREMENTS

LEGO pieces are described by the number of studs on them. If a brick has 2 studs across and 3 up, it's a 2x3 brick. If a piece is tall, it has a third number that is its height in standard bricks. Bricks are three times taller than LEGO plates.

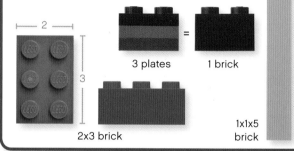

3 plates = 1 brick

2x3 brick

1x1x5 brick

STUD

Round raised bumps on top of bricks and plates are called studs. A chain has a single stud at each end. Studs fit into "tubes," which are on the bottom of bricks and plates.

2x2 corner plate

LEGO chain with two end studs

CLIP

Some pieces have clips on them. You can fit other elements into these clips. Pieces such as ladders fasten onto bars using built-in clips.

Ladder with two clips

 1x1 plate with clip

 1x1 plate with clip

 2x3 tile with clips

BAR

Bars are useful for building long, thin features, but are also used with clips to create angles and moving parts. Bars are the perfect size to fit minifigure hands and some holes.

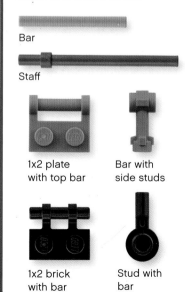

Bar

Staff

1x2 plate with top bar

Bar with side studs

1x2 brick with bar

Stud with bar

TECHNIC ELEMENTS

LEGO® Technic pieces make it easy to include working features in your builds. Combine gears and axles to bring your builds to life, or simply add them to your models to recreate the look of your favorite *Star Wars* movie set designs.

LEGO Technic half pin with bar

LEGO Technic angle connector

LEGO Technic axle

LEGO Technic friction pin

LEGO Technic half pin

LEGO Technic axle pin

LEGO Technic axle with notches

TILE

When you want a smooth finish to your build, you need to use a tile. Printed tiles add extra detail to your models.

1x1 printed tile

1x6 tile

2x2 tile

2x2 tile with pin

2x3 shield tile

SIDEWAYS BUILDING

Sometimes you need to build in two directions. That's when you need bricks or plates like these, with studs on more than one side.

1x4 brick with side studs

1x1 brick with side studs

1x1 brick with side stud

1x2/2x2 angle plate

PLATE

Like bricks, plates have studs on top and tubes on the bottom. However, plates are much thinner than bricks. Studs on jumper plates are placed slightly across to allow centered details.

1x8 plate with side rail

1x2 jumper plate

1x2 plate with bar

1x1 round plate

4x4 curved plate

2x4 plate

4x4 round plate

2x4 angled plate

BRICK

Where would a builder be without the brick? It's the basis of most models and it comes in a huge variety of shapes and sizes.

1x4 arched brick

1x1 headlight brick

2x2 brick

2x2 domed brick

SLOPE

Slopes are bigger at the bottom than on top. Inverted slopes are the same, but upside down. They are smaller at the bottom and bigger on top.

1x2 slope

1x1 slope

1x2 Inverted slope

SPECIAL PIECES

Special pieces are used to create specific structures, or to link the build to a LEGO theme. Decorative pieces like these all work well in the LEGO *Star Wars* world.

Harpoon piece

Ice cream piece

Curved slope brick

Plate with octagonal ring

JOINT

If you want to make a roof that opens or give a creature a tail that moves, you need a moving part, such as a hinge or other joint.

2x2 brick with ball joint

Ball joint socket

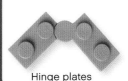

Hinge plates

1x2 hinge brick and 1x2 hinge plate

CHAPTER 1
NABOO

AMIDALA'S ORDERS

On peaceful Naboo, Queen Amidala is celebrating. An invasion by battle droids has been defeated! But the danger is not quite over. Jenn Smeel, one of the Queen's loyal guards, brings news that a squad of droids is still active and advancing on the Royal Palace! The Queen tells Smeel he must find a way to stop them.

THE DROIDS ARE ON THEIR WAY!

BRIEFING ROOM
Located within the Royal Palace, Queen Amidala's briefing room is a dignified space with elegant archways, columns, and scrolls. It looks out to the beautiful blue waters that cover much of Naboo's surface.

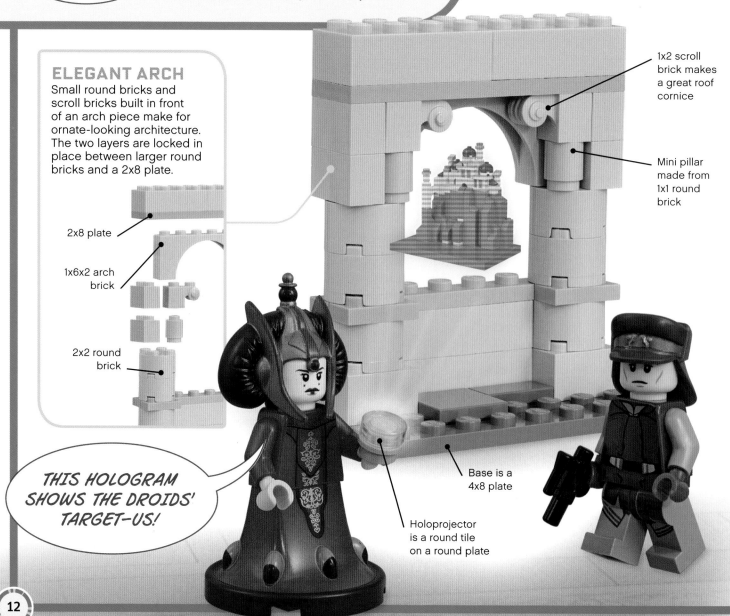

ELEGANT ARCH
Small round bricks and scroll bricks built in front of an arch piece make for ornate-looking architecture. The two layers are locked in place between larger round bricks and a 2x8 plate.

2x8 plate

1x6x2 arch brick

2x2 round brick

1x2 scroll brick makes a great roof cornice

Mini pillar made from 1x1 round brick

Base is a 4x8 plate

Holoprojector is a round tile on a round plate

THIS HOLOGRAM SHOWS THE DROIDS' TARGET—US!

NABOO HOLOGRAM

Naboo's Royal Palace perches high on a cliff in the capital city of Theed, where the snaking Solleu River becomes a dramatic waterfall. This microscale version is built on a base of sideways blue bricks.

WHAT WILL YOU BUILD?

- Microscale Theed streets
- Palace guardroom
- Royal treasury

PILLAR BOX

The palace's microscale columns are made from rows of 1x1 bricks with bars. Smooth tiles sit beneath the bars, where pieces with studs would not fit. Tiles are used elsewhere for a smooth exterior.

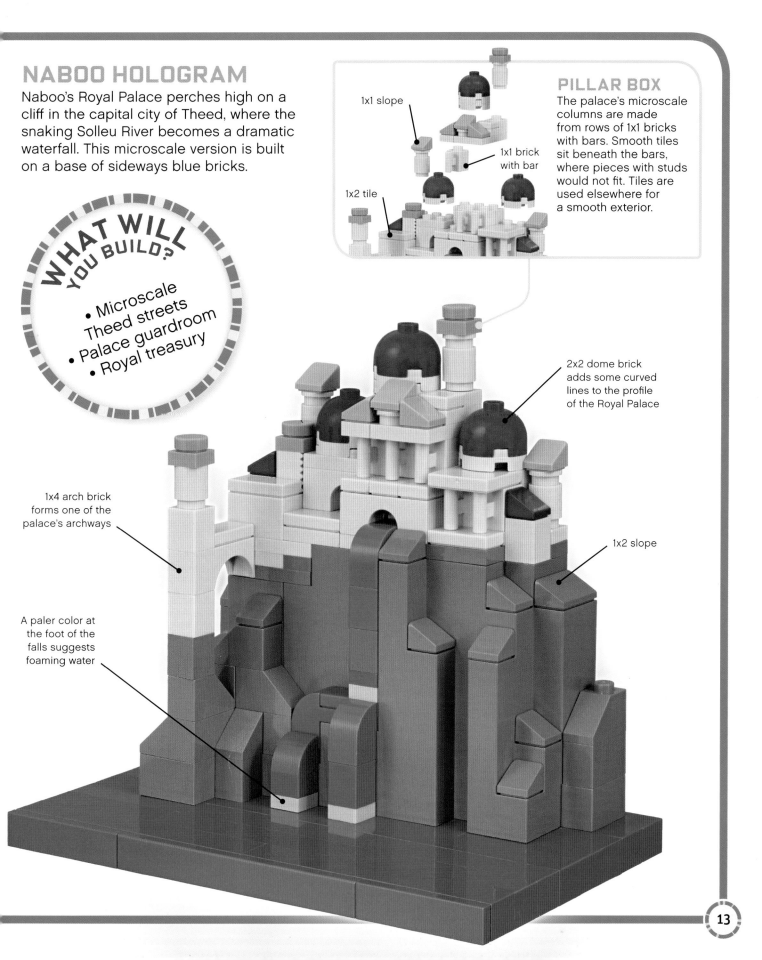

1x1 slope

1x1 brick with bar

1x2 tile

2x2 dome brick adds some curved lines to the profile of the Royal Palace

1x4 arch brick forms one of the palace's archways

1x2 slope

A paler color at the foot of the falls suggests foaming water

PALACE PASSAGE

Smeel knows the palace well, but only the Queen holds all its secrets! In the throne room, she shows him a hidden passage that leads to the underwater city of Otoh Gunga. It has just been built to mark the Queen's new friendship with the Gungans. Smeel can use the passage to bypass the droids and get help for his mission.

I'VE GOT TO GET TO OTOH GUNGA!

THRONE ROOM

The Queen's throne is a courtly but comfy chair, flanked by fluted columns. It is built on a raised platform, so everyone must look up to the Queen—even when she is sitting down!

THRONE APART

The sweeping sides of the throne are made from sideways wheel arch pieces. They fit onto headlight bricks and follow the curve of a 4x4 round plate.

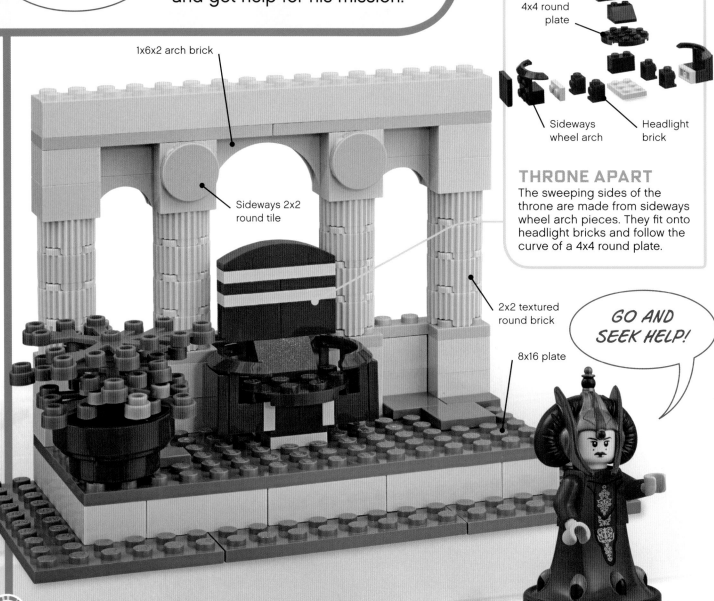

1x6x2 arch brick

Sideways 2x2 round tile

4x4 round plate

Sideways wheel arch

Headlight brick

2x2 textured round brick

8x16 plate

GO AND SEEK HELP!

FRONT VIEW

All-gray minifigure
as statue

SECRET PASSAGE

The Royal Palace is full of hidden doors to secret passageways. This one looks like a recess for a statue when it is closed, but it swings open on a pair of hinge plates, to reveal a secret entrance!

BUILD FOR STEALTH

• • •

• Make builds look like they have just one purpose
• Hide a second purpose behind decorative features
• Try to make joins for moving parts invisible

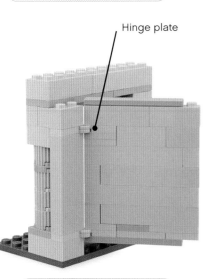

Hinge plate

REAR VIEW

1x8x2 arch brick

2x2 round plate

2x2 plate

Smooth base of the secret doorway made from 2x2 tiles

WHERE WILL THIS PASSAGE LEAD?

Turbine piece

MEET THE GUNGANS

Just when Smeel thinks the tunnel will never end, it opens out to a watery chamber, where a submarine is ready to take him to the heart of Otoh Gunga. In one of the city's bubble-domed buildings, he meets with the Gungans and they agree to help him stop the droids. Together, they head back toward the palace.

WE'RE PLEASED TO MEET YOU!

GUNGAN SUB

The Gungans are powerful swimmers, but also get around their underwater world in strange submarines called bongos. This one has a bubble cockpit and trailing tentacles made from tail pieces.

THIS BONGO IS FAR FROM SUB-STANDARD!

One of three tail tip pieces, which suggest motion through the water

Sideways LEGO Technic gear rack

SUB SIDES AND TAIL

The sloping fins on the sides of the sub pivot on hinges made from clips and bars. The raylike tail sections fit onto a 1x4 brick with holes.

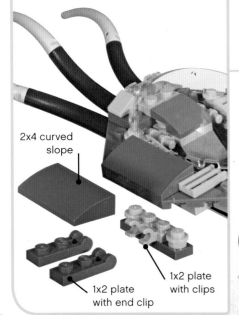

2x4 curved slope

1x2 plate with clips

1x2 plate with end clip

BUILD FOR MOVING IN WATER

• Use flowing shapes to glide through water
• Add joints and hinges for fishlike flexibility
• Keep builds slim or flat, with tapered ends

OTOH GUNGA BUILDING

Deep beneath the waters of Naboo, the buildings of Otoh Gunga use bubblelike force fields to keep their occupants safe and dry. This one has large windows looking out to an underwater garden.

8x8 dome attaches to the building with a hinge brick

2x2 grooved brick

REAR VIEW

TWO-PIPE SOLUTION

The air circulation system on the outside of the building is made from exhaust pipe pieces. They are held securely by bricks with holes at one end, and sit loosely in the same kind of brick at the other end.

1x1 brick with hole

Exhaust pipe piece

WE HAVE A VISITOR!

Grass piece

Whip piece doubles as exotic underwater vegetation

Sea grass piece

1x1 plate with top clip

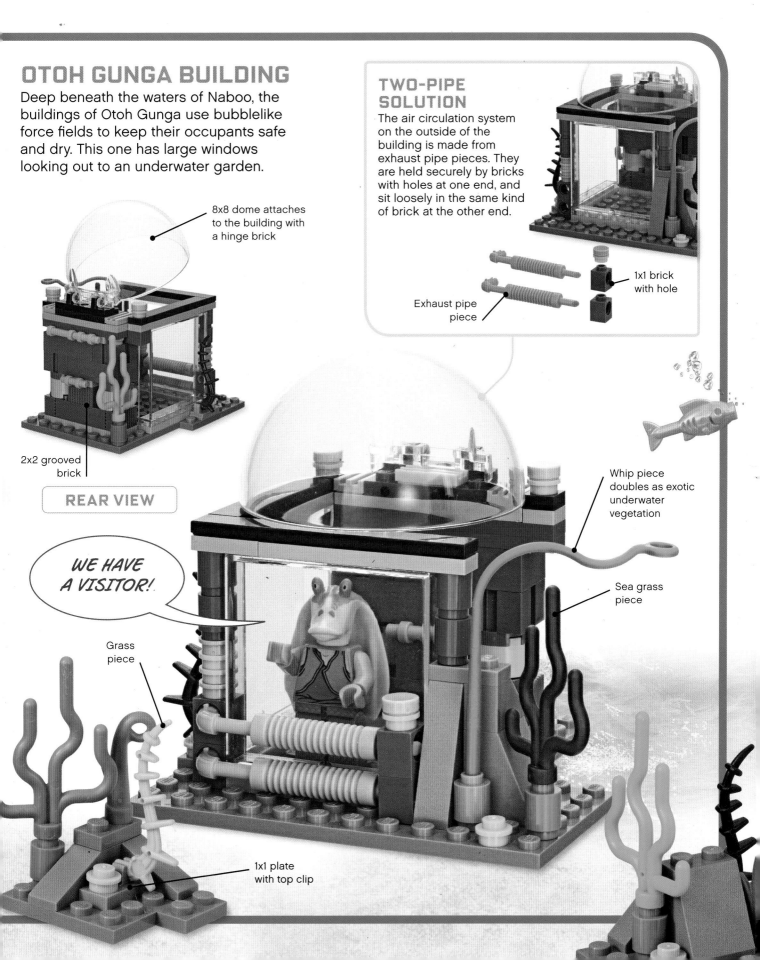

SHORELINE ATTACK

Smeel takes the sub all the way back to the edge of the palace grounds, and his new friends swim beside him. Coming ashore by the palace walls, they spy battle droids—including one flying straight for them on an attack skimmer! The Gungans draw the skimmer's fire as Smeel sees what he must do to defeat the droids.

OUT OF COLD WATER INTO HOT!

WHAT WILL YOU BUILD?
- Royal Palace fountain
- Battle droid cannon
- Royal Palace gates

1x6x2 arch brick creates an elegant span of the palace wall

PALACE TREES

Neatly tended trees line the formal gardens of the Royal Palace. As well as looking pretty, they make great cover for anyone trying to avoid fire from a battle droid skimmer!

Gray and tan pieces look like stone

PILE OF LEAVES

Each tree is made of stacked plant pieces with a bar running through them for strength. The bar continues down into the trunk, which gets larger to help it stand.

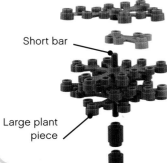

Short bar

Large plant piece

ENEMY UP IN THE SKY!

PALACE WALLS

This stretch of the Royal Palace's outer walls includes a statue on a plinth that is built separately. Building in small, freestanding sections makes it easy to arrange (and rearrange) much longer walls.

2x2 jumper plate

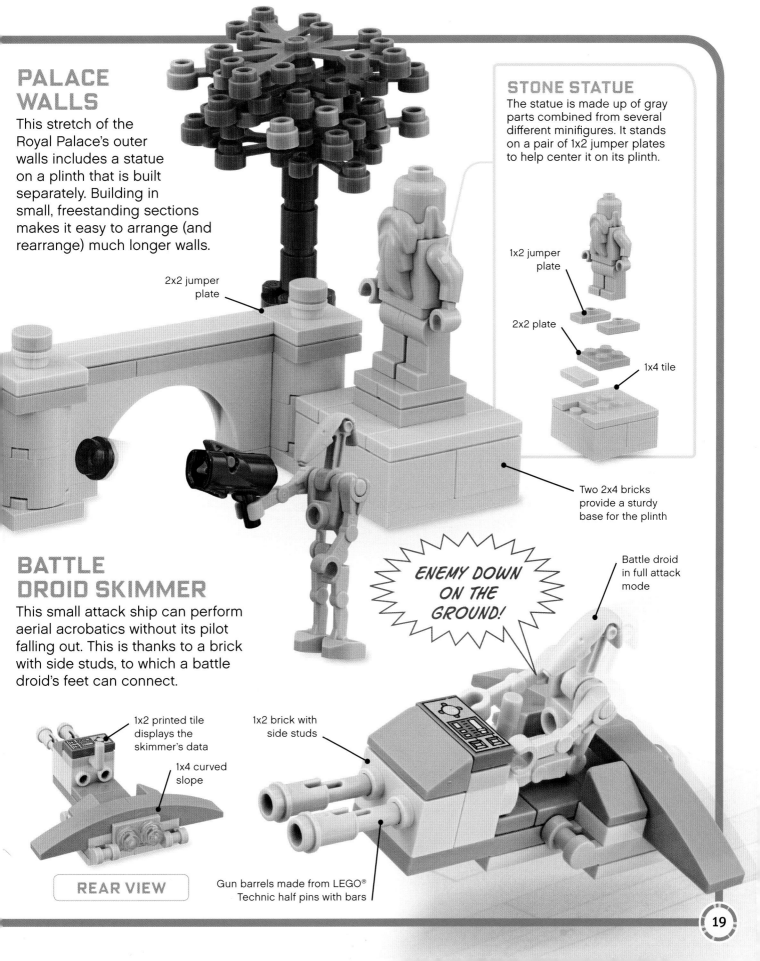

STONE STATUE

The statue is made up of gray parts combined from several different minifigures. It stands on a pair of 1x2 jumper plates to help center it on its plinth.

1x2 jumper plate

2x2 plate

1x4 tile

Two 2x4 bricks provide a sturdy base for the plinth

BATTLE DROID SKIMMER

This small attack ship can perform aerial acrobatics without its pilot falling out. This is thanks to a brick with side studs, to which a battle droid's feet can connect.

ENEMY DOWN ON THE GROUND!

Battle droid in full attack mode

1x2 printed tile displays the skimmer's data

1x4 curved slope

1x2 brick with side studs

REAR VIEW

Gun barrels made from LEGO® Technic half pins with bars

19

SWAMPY STEALTH

Spotting the drop pod that's controlling the droids, Smeel races toward it, only to find himself face to face with a droid battle tank! It fires, he ducks—and the blast flies straight over his head, destroying the droid control pod! In an instant, all the droids shut down, and Naboo is safe once more. Mission accomplished!

> MY ENERGY LEVELS HAVE TAKEN A DIP!

TOP ANTENNA

The antenna on top of the pod is made from a minifigure harpoon, which slots into a 1x1 cone and a 1x1 round brick. A small radar dish slots onto the handle.

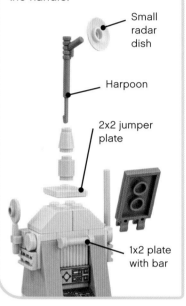

Small radar dish

Harpoon

2x2 jumper plate

1x2 plate with bar

DROP POD

Battle droids are usually remotely controlled from a huge spaceship, but this squad is powered by an experimental drop pod. Its antenna sends orders to the droids, and its inner workings are protected by folding armor panels.

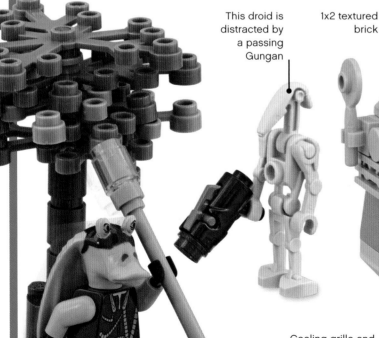

This droid is distracted by a passing Gungan

1x2 textured brick

2x3 tile with clips serves as a protective panel for the pod

> THE PLUG'S BEEN PULLED ON THIS PODCAST!

Cooling grille and accessories attach to studs on a downward angle plate

WHAT WILL YOU BUILD?

- Carnivorous plants
- Droid transporter
- Medal ceremony

CAMBYLICTUS TREE

The Royal Palace grounds are full of rare and unusual trees, including this huge Cambylictus, which can only grow in water. Its trunk is built from slope bricks and half arch pieces.

Large plant piece makes a perfect canopy for the towering Cambylictus

1x3x3 half arch

1x3 slope brick adds rigidity to the trunk

Water represented by blue 6x6 plate

TAKE THAT, SMEE-E-EL ... ZZZZZ!

BATTLE TANK

This AAT (Armored Assault Tank) glides along on a repulsorlift base, firing a pair of powerful laser cannons. There is space for a droid pilot to operate the controls at the back.

Cannons made from LEGO Technic pins with stud ends

1x2 slope

2x2 corner slope brick

TANK TOP TO TOE

The base of the tank is built sideways, using bricks with side studs to connect it to the main hull. The cannons rotate on LEGO Technic friction pins in bricks with holes.

LEGO Technic friction pin

Round brick with hole

Sideways 1x4 brick with side studs

CHAPTER 2
CORELLIA

UNDER ORDERS

On the grim factory world of Corellia, two young friends called Han and Qi'ra have no choice but to work for the White Worm crime gang. One day, they hope to escape, but for now they take their orders from the mysterious Moloch. Today, he wants them to steal a valuable cloud car from a well-guarded Imperial compound!

CALL YOURSELVES WORMS, YOU RATS?!

BRIEFING ROOM

The Den of the White Worms is a maze of murky corridors beneath Corellia's Coronet City. This arch suggests the shape of the corridor beyond. Beware the Corellian hounds that lurk in the passages!

1x6x2 arch

Smooth 1x2 tiles lock the arch in place at the top

Corellian hound

THIS IS NO SOLO MISSION!

GRAY ARCH

Gather small and unusual pieces in a single shade of gray to build realistic-looking industrial details. Pieces with bars and other round sections are particularly good for making pipework.

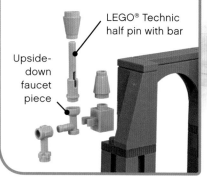

LEGO® Technic half pin with bar

Upside-down faucet piece

CORELLIA HOLOGRAM

Huge factories hug the coast of industrial Corellia, giving the planet a gray and gloomy look. Using pieces of mostly one color but lots of different shapes is a clever way to build a microscale factory.

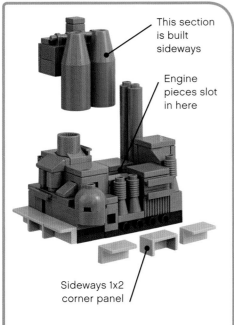

This section is built sideways

Engine pieces slot in here

Sideways 1x2 corner panel

FACTORY OUTPUT

The two large smokestacks are sideways jet engine pieces that slot into the factory's center. This upper part of the build rests on the lower section on plates rather than connecting to it via studs.

WHAT WILL YOU BUILD?

- White Worm leader, Lady Proxima
- Proxima's chamber
- Han's home

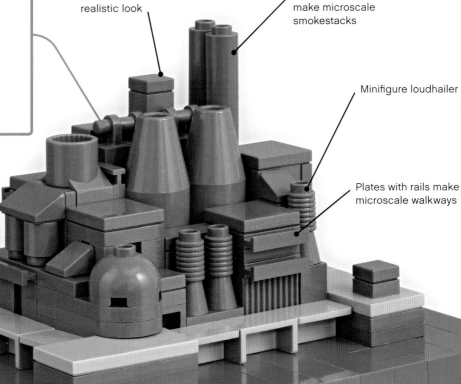

Smooth tiles cover studs for a more realistic look

1x1x6 columns make microscale smokestacks

Minifigure loudhailer

Plates with rails make microscale walkways

Both corner towers are centered on 2x2 jumper plates

RACE AGAINST TIME

Han and Qi'ra are under orders not to waste time, so they race to the compound in a pair of speeders. Han can't help driving a little too fast, and they soon attract the attention of an Imperial traffic officer! To escape, they lead the officer into a maze of factories that only a Coronet local can navigate at speed.

LET'S GOOOOOOOO!

FACTORY WALL

This wall section includes lots of elements of a factory using just a few pieces. The pipes are made from different bar pieces, while textured bricks make realistic cooling vents.

1x2 plate with bar

Long bar slots into vertical bar with side studs

1x2 textured brick serves as a horizontal cooling vent

SMOOTH RIDES

Both the Imperial speeder and Qi'ra's speeder have smooth sides built out from two rows of angle plates. Use a smooth tile to make the stripe along the side.

Wheel arch

Three 1x2/2x2 angle plates

1x6 tile

2x2 tile

SPEEDERS AREN'T FOR SPEEDING!

A 1x2 printed tile makes a dashboard

1x2 plate with rail

IMPERIAL SPEEDER

On Corellia, people drive landspeeders instead of cars. Speeders come in all shapes and sizes, and many different colors. The Imperial speeders are nearly always gloomy shades of gray!

BUILD FOR
SPEED
- Use curves and smooth parts to make your build more aerodynamic
- Make the front thinner than the back to cut through the air

ROUND THE CORNERS

The rounded sides of Han's speeder are made from ridged curved slope bricks and small curved half arches, all of which are built on sideways using angle plates.

1x2/2x2 angle plate

Curved slope brick

1x3 tile

Curved half arch

Silver pieces add engine detail

HAN'S SPEEDER

Han's stylish speeder has moving controls made from claw pieces that clip onto a plate with a bar. Smooth slide plates underneath allow it to glide along any surface.

Printed 2x2 ring tile looks like moving fan blades

1x2 curved half arch

Slide plate

UNDERSIDE VIEW

Two sideways 1x3 curved slopes

SO SLOW DOWN, OFFICER!

1x2 jumper plate provides a base for the driver's console

QI'RA'S SPEEDER

A more colorful version of the Imperial speeder, Qi'ra's ride uses 1x3 curved slopes to give it a streamlined appearance. A top stripe is centered on jumper plates.

PIERSIDE PLOT

After losing the trooper in the grimy back streets, Han and Qi'ra burst into the city docks. The only sign of life here is a fellow local fishing for his lunch, so the pair make a plan to steal the cloud car. Han says it won't be easy to get past the guards, but Qi'ra says that the fisherman has given her an idea ...

TIME FOR A NICE QUIET ... WHO'S HERE?

CORELLIA DOCKS

The industrial landscape of Corellia spills out to the sea at the docks. This section of pier is reached through a sliding door, which Han squeezes his speeder through!

Upside-down 1x2 plate with end bar

Tube with clip

1x1 brick with clip

I THINK WE'RE OFF THE HOOK ...

Lights can be angled

BRIGHT IDEA
Line the docks with a row of lights made by using bars and clips. Build them into a wall at the base so they can't be easily knocked over.

Floor sections are made from 8x8 lattice plates

28

WHAT WILL YOU BUILD?

- Security checkpoint
- Cargo freighter
- Loading crane

BEHIND THE DOOR

The sliding door moves back and forth behind the dock wall on smooth plates with rails. The wall is thicker at both ends to stop the door from moving too far.

2x8 plate with rails

Axle pin connects to LEGO Technic tube

Projecting brick serves as a handle

Fishing rod is actually a whip piece

Han and Qi'ra's speeders are just narrow enough to fit through the sliding door

... AND SO ARE THESE FISH!

Transparent and blue pieces represent water

PIPE LINES

The curved pipes in the dock walls are made from LEGO Technic tubes and axle connectors, held together with axle pins. Bricks with cross-holes secure them to the wall.

Axle pin

Curved tube

LEGO Technic axle connector

FISHY BUSINESS

Qi'ra arrives at the Imperial compound on her own. She can see the cloud car just inside the security gate—and lots of guards on the outside! She walks right up to the guards, armed not with a blaster, but with a delicious piece of fish, which she eats right in front of them. The guards are suddenly all very hungry!

I'LL SEE YOU SOON, QI'RA!

COMPOUND WALL

Use large pieces such as girders to build a simple, strong wall. Then use smaller pieces for decoration. Add depth at the base of the wall for stability.

1x2 inverted slope brick creates angular overhang

1x6x5 girder

Light made from 1x1 round red tile set in 1x2 brick with hole

I CAN SMELL SOMETHING FISHY ...

BUILD FOR STRENGTH
• • •
- Use large pieces to build a strong wall
- Build up from a sturdy base—all buildings need solid foundations
- Lock pieces in place with a secure top

COMPOUND GATE

Build the top half and the bottom half of the gateway separately and then join the two sections at the narrowest point. This will be easier than trying to build the roof on last.

2x12 plate is the main structure at the top of the gate

1x1 printed tile with Imperial badge

PIN-ON BADGE

The Imperial badge above the gate is connected to a brick with a hole using a LEGO Technic half pin. The lights on the compound wall (far left) attach in the same way.

2x4 tile

LEGO Technic half pin

1x2 brick with hole

2x12 plate

Stud shooter serves as security light

Stud shooter on cloud car

2x2x3 slope bricks on either side provide the gateway's structural base

Two 1x4 printed tiles create a hazard strip for the gateway

JUST HOW I LIKE IT—ON THE DARK SIDE!

THIS FISH IS COOKED PERFECTLY!

HAN BURGERS

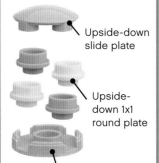

The Imperial guards can't take it any longer! They ask Qi'ra where she got the fish, and she directs them to a traveling food stall that Han has set up nearby. The troopers rush to try his Corellian cod burger—so Qi'ra sneaks into the compound and flies off with the cloud car. Mission accomplished!

REEL THEM IN, HAN!

FAST FOOD

Use an upside-down 2x2 ring as the base of your burger bun (or as a food plate), and it will slot onto the top of a minifigure's upright hand.

Upside-down slide plate

Upside-down 1x1 round plate

Upside-down 2x2 ring

Green 1x1 round plate for lettuce

CORELLIAN COD BURGER

Built entirely using upside-down pieces, this burger is topped with a slide plate—more commonly used on the underside of ships. You can add as many layers of filling as you like!

CAN YOU HEAR A CLOUD CAR TAKING OFF?

THAT'S JUST MY STOMACH RUMBLING!

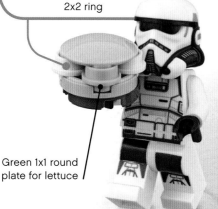

Heavy duty stormtrooper gun

FOOD STALL

Han's street food stall has a huge fish-shaped sign to attract customers. There is also a cooking area and a counter where customers pick up their orders and add their favorite sauces.

1x1 slope

1x2 slope brick

1x1 ring

1x1 cone

2x2 round brick

4x4 round plate

SCALE MODEL

The fish sign is made from a mix of slopes, curved slopes, and plates. It is built onto a post made from a long bar with a 1x1 ring on top and a 1x1 cone at the base.

WHAT WILL YOU BUILD?
• Customer seating
• Fish pie
• Vegetarian option

1x3 curved slope

Create a strong lower jaw bone for the fish with a 1x4 inverted curved slope

Long bar and cone attaches to a 2x2 round brick to make a stable base

2x2 jumper plate

1x2/1x2 angle plate

PAN SOLO

Han's cooking station has three heaters. Two are round printed tiles, while the one that is in use is a "red-hot" round plate to which a pan piece can be attached.

THE EMPIRE LIKES SNACKS!

Mustard and ketchup dispensers to add to the burgers

Han's table top is mainly made up of 2x2 tiles

1x2 printed tile displays oven controls and dials

CHAPTER 3
SCARIF

SEND IN ZIN!

The Rebel Alliance is on high alert! Something strange is happening on the tropical Imperial world of Scarif, and the rebels want to know what. Wise old Admiral Ackbar summons the ace pilot Zin and tells him to investigate the planet. He says it will be a great chance for Zin to test his new experimental Y-wing fighter!

I SENSE SOMETHING FISHY!

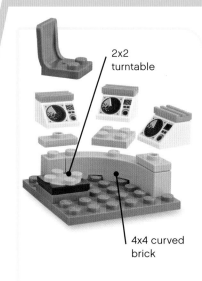

2x2 turntable

4x4 curved brick

SCREEN TIME
Ackbar can monitor Zin's progress on three screens that angle toward him on single studs. His chair is built onto a turntable, so it can move in any direction.

BRIEFING ROOM
Compared to the might of the Empire, the Rebel Alliance is a ragtag force, reliant on basic equipment. Admiral Ackbar's briefing room is a simple affair, made from fewer than 20 pieces.

TAKE A GOOD LOOK AT SCARIF!

2x2 printed slope brick with display screens and dials

I THOUGHT IT WOULD BE BIGGER!

6x6 plate

SIMPLE CITADEL

The tall Citadel Tower dominates this build. It is built from a 1x1x5 column and other round pieces, flanked by 1x2x3 slope bricks that are slightly offset using jumper plates.

Small radar dish

Harpoon

1x2x3 slope brick

Green and brown round plates make microscale trees

SCARIF HOLOGRAM

Small, sandy islands dot the bright blue waters of Scarif. It would be a paradise if they weren't linked by grim Imperial buildings! This microscale Scarif is built on a sideways base.

1x1 round brick provides base for the radar dish

1x1x5 column

Bridge made from 1x6 tile

WHAT WILL YOU BUILD?
- Rebel target range
- Ackbar's quarters
- Launch bay doors

BUILDING THE BASE

The watery base upon which Scarif's islands lie is made from blue bricks smoothed off with tiles. The structure also includes three 1x4 bricks with side studs, to which the islands are attached.

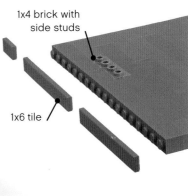

1x4 brick with side studs

1x6 tile

SUB, SEA, AND SAND

The sun is shining as Zin flies his Y-wing down to the beaches and oceans of Scarif. He sees stormtroopers everywhere, but they are not marching or training—they are sunbathing! To get a closer look, he activates his ship's unique function, turning it into a submarine that can approach the shore without being seen.

MY Y-WING HAS WATER WINGS!

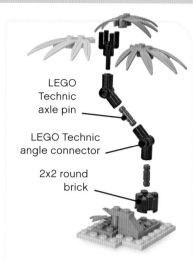

LEGO Technic axle pin

LEGO Technic angle connector

2x2 round brick

PALM READING
Use LEGO® Technic angle connectors and axle pins to make a twisting tree trunk. Secure it to a sandy base build using a 2x2 round brick.

Bright green finger leaf piece

BEACH SCENE
As well as a palm tree, this beach scene includes sun loungers, a sound system, and stormtroopers! Each lounger is six studs long, to accommodate a minifigure's full length.

AAH! THE EMPIRE KICKS BACK!

1x1 round brick with leaves adds extra foliage to the scene

1x2 tiles create patterned bed

2x6 plate forms part of the sandy base

RETRO RADIO
This retro sound system looks just like the real thing, only much smaller! It has round tiles for speakers and a phone receiver as a handle.

Printed 1x1 round tile

REBEL Y-SUB

Just like a normal Y-wing starfighter, Zin's ship has two large engines for space flight. What makes his ship extra special is its pair of spinning turbines that also enable it to travel underwater!

2x6 plate

Sideways 1x1 brick with side studs

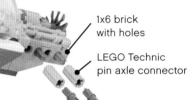

UNDERSIDE VIEW

WHAT WILL YOU BUILD?

• Lifeguard station
• Beach barbecue
• Surf trooper

Blue 1x1 ring serves as the periscope lens

Long bar

MY PERISCOPE LETS ME SEE MORE OF THE SEA SHORE!

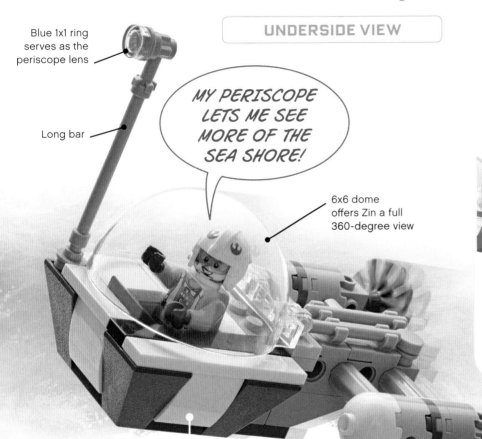

6x6 dome offers Zin a full 360-degree view

HOLES IN THE HULL

The rear hull of the Y-wing is made from two 1x6 bricks with holes. LEGO Technic parts connect these to the engines, which are built using sideways round bricks with holes.

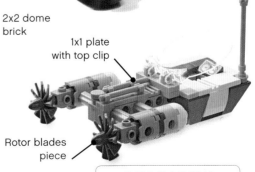

1x6 brick with holes

LEGO Technic pin axle connector

Sideways 2x2 round brick with holes

2x2 dome brick

UNDER THE DOME

The Y-wing's cockpit is built around a 6x6x2 inverted corner slope brick. Sideways curved slopes complete the sides, and smooth tiles cover the top.

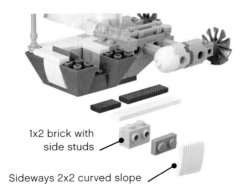

1x2 brick with side studs

Sideways 2x2 curved slope

1x1 plate with top clip

Rotor blades piece

REAR VIEW

39

TROOPER SNOOPER

Leaving his ship underwater, Zin sneaks onto the beach and listens in on the conversation of two stormtroopers who are buying ice cream. He overhears them saying that someone very important is taking their annual vacation here. But before he can learn any more, Zin has to hide from an Imperial land and sea patrol!

WHO COULD THE VIP BE?

ICE BOX
The ice cream stall is built almost entirely using sideways parts held in place with a clip. Only the parasol is upright.

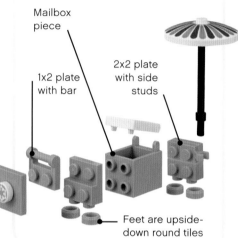

Mailbox piece

2x2 plate with side studs

1x2 plate with bar

Feet are upside-down round tiles

ICE CREAM STAND
Beneath a palm tree (built like the one on p.38), a friendly Bith sells ice cream to the stormtroopers on Scarif. His stall has a built-in chest freezer to keep the frozen treats cold.

Palm leaf piece provides shade for the ice cream seller

I HOPE HE'S TALKING TO HIS POPSICLE!

HEY YOU, FREEZE!

Ice cream piece

Imperial emblem

IMPERIAL HOVERCRAFT

Hovercraft can travel on land or water. They are lifted slightly above the surface by a cushion of air blasted out from the base. This Imperial model patrols the shores of Scarif on the lookout for spies!

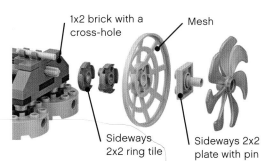

1x2 brick with a cross-hole

Mesh

Sideways 2x2 ring tile

Sideways 2x2 plate with pin

BEHIND THE SPIN

Rotor blades at the back of the craft spin on a sideways plate with a pin beneath. A mesh to protect the pilot fits onto a LEGO Technic axle in a brick with a cross-hole.

Hovercraft dials on printed slope tile

Stud shooter

REAR VIEW

2x2x4 curved brick makes a smooth front

Cushion made from four 4x4 round bricks with holes

IMPERIAL WALKER

This one-person walker is a scaled-down version of the Empire's mighty AT-ATs. The pilot's elevated viewpoint and the walker's head-mounted blasters provide vital support for the fast-moving hovercraft patrols.

I WISH I HAD AN ICE CREAM!

Head pivots on clip-and-bar hinge

Tiles give the walker a smooth body

1x1 round tile

Bar with side studs

Upside-down 1x1 tile

MINI AT-AT

The walker's four legs connect to two plates with bars. Each leg is made from a bar with side studs, and an upside-down tile for a foot.

ZIN IN THE SWIM

Zin races to hide behind a palm tree but runs straight into a stormtrooper, knocking over his sandcastles! The trooper raises the alarm, and two missiles are fired in Zin's direction from a nearby bunker. As he jumps into the sea, Zin spots the vacationing VIP heading straight for him on a Jet Ski!

I'D EVEN MADE A SAND DEATH STAR!

BUILD FOR TARGETING

- Build a pivot to hit targets at different distances
- Use pins to hold the pivot in position
- Always aim away from yourself and others

Canopy made from palm tree pieces that clip onto a brick with four angled bars

Incoming missile fired from bunker launcher

SANDCASTLES SCENE

This scene makes use of the same palm tree design seen on p.38. It is also used on the facing page. You could build a whole oasis of palm trees, or use the same one again and again!

LEGO Technic trunk

MY LOVELY SANDCASTLES!

Minifigure shovel

Sandcastles are 1x1 bricks

I'VE REALLY PUT MY FOOT IN IT!

1x1 round brick with leaves

Minifigure bucket, essential for making sandcastles

GET BACK HERE, YOU SAND BLASTER!

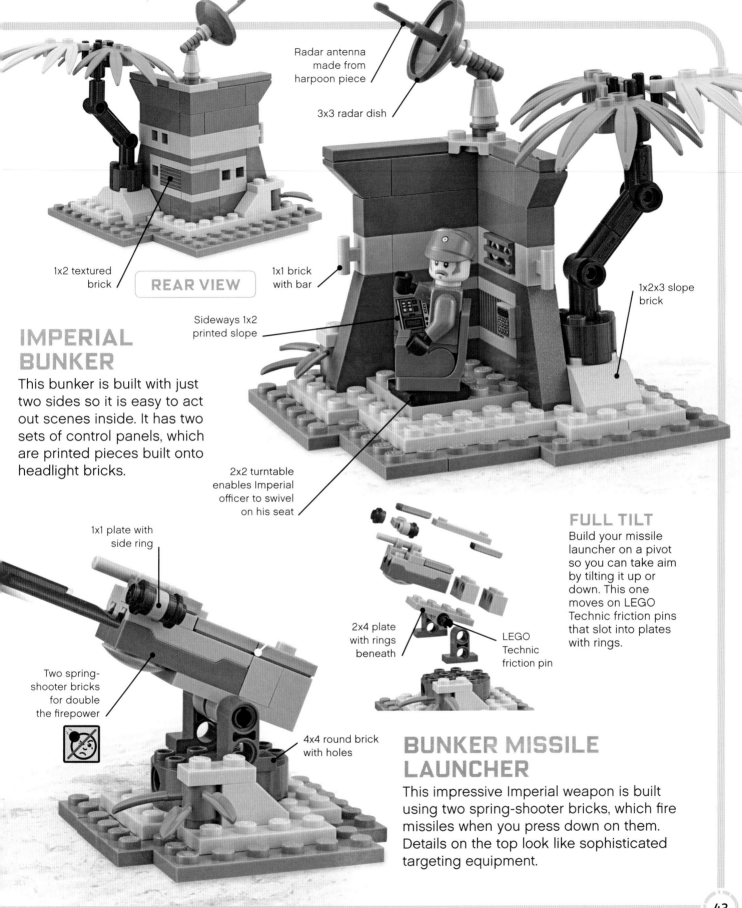

Radar antenna made from harpoon piece

3x3 radar dish

1x2 textured brick

REAR VIEW

1x1 brick with bar

Sideways 1x2 printed slope

1x2x3 slope brick

IMPERIAL BUNKER

This bunker is built with just two sides so it is easy to act out scenes inside. It has two sets of control panels, which are printed pieces built onto headlight bricks.

2x2 turntable enables Imperial officer to swivel on his seat

1x1 plate with side ring

Two spring-shooter bricks for double the firepower

4x4 round brick with holes

2x4 plate with rings beneath

LEGO Technic friction pin

FULL TILT

Build your missile launcher on a pivot so you can take aim by tilting it up or down. This one moves on LEGO Technic friction pins that slot into plates with rings.

BUNKER MISSILE LAUNCHER

This impressive Imperial weapon is built using two spring-shooter bricks, which fire missiles when you press down on them. Details on the top look like sophisticated targeting equipment.

MAKING WAVES

Zin can't believe it—the Jet Skier is Darth Vader, followed by a flying guard! With the missiles still on his tail, Zin swims straight for the Jet Ski. The missiles lock onto it and explode, throwing Zin back to his Y-wing! He flies off, leaving an angry Vader flailing in the water. The Imperial vacation is ended. Mission accomplished!

TAKE A BATH, VADER!

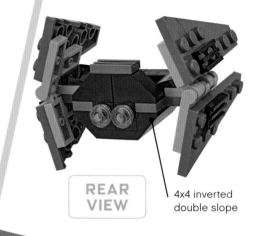

REAR VIEW

4x4 inverted double slope

TIE INTERCEPTOR

Even when he's on holiday, Darth Vader keeps his personal guard close at hand. With its aerodynamic solar collector wings, this TIE Interceptor can shadow his every move on Scarif—no matter how fast!

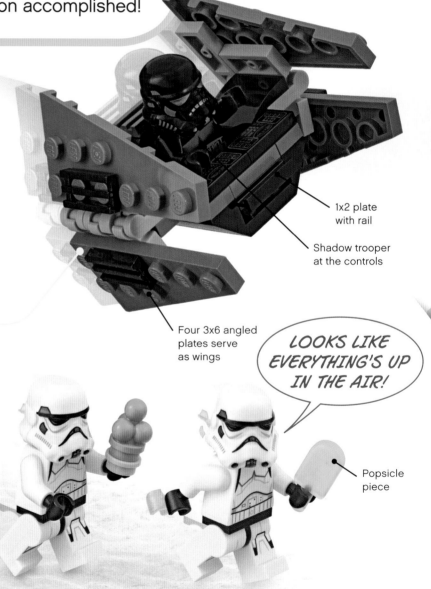

1x2 plate with rail

Shadow trooper at the controls

Four 3x6 angled plates serve as wings

LOOKS LIKE EVERYTHING'S UP IN THE AIR!

Popsicle piece

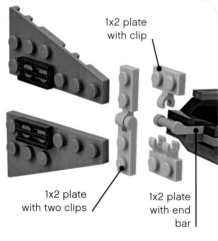

1x2 plate with clip

1x2 plate with two clips

1x2 plate with end bar

CLIP YOUR WINGS
The Interceptor's angled wings connect to the main hull using hinges made from clips and bars. A second clip-and-bar connection adds strength at the back on each side.

VADER'S JET SKI

Inspired by the shape of Darth Vader's own Star Destroyer, this speedy Jet Ski slices through the waters of Scarif. Piloting it is Vader's favorite vacation pastime!

SO LONG, SCARIF!

MY JET SKI'S GOING TO CRAAAASH …!

WHAT WILL YOU BUILD?

- Imperial dune buggy
- Scarif sea monster
- Vader's beach hut

Blue 1x1 round plate

Main hull made from 4x6 inverted curved slope

UNDERNEATH VIEW

1x2 plate with clip to attach the handlebars

2x4 double angled plate

CHAPTER 4
BESPIN

GUARD DUTY

Sooner or later, everyone comes to Cloud City, the huge mining station that hangs in the sky above the planet Bespin. Today's newest arrival is the tough bounty hunter Bossk, who has stolen a barrel meant for station boss Lando Calrissian. So Lando calls in his top guard, Seb, and briefs him to get the goods back!

I'M THE BOSS HERE, NOT BOSSK!

LEARNING CURVES
The rounded sides of the briefing room start with curved plates, then curved bricks and panel pieces. The window is a single piece set back behind the top of the one straight wall.

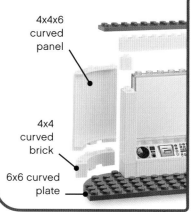

4x4x6 curved panel

4x4 curved brick

6x6 curved plate

BRIEFING ROOM

Cloud City is an ultramodern station with gleaming curved walls and wide windows for admiring the skies over Bespin. Lando has an especially good view of the clouds from his private office and briefing room.

A single 2x12 plate secures the walls at the top

The recessed window adds a sense of depth

GOOD TO SEE YOU, SEB!

ALWAYS READY TO HELP, LANDO!

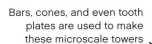

CLOUD CITY HOLOGRAM

Shaped like a giant floating mushroom, Cloud City has a circular main section with a long "stalk" piercing the cloud level below. The gleaming white towers on top are the key feature of this microscale version.

TINY TOWERS

When you build in microscale, even the smallest piece can be a skyscraper! Short bars make slender towers, tooth plates make pointed spires, and a faucet piece makes a walkway to the center tower.

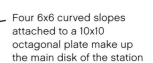

Short bar in 1x1 round brick

1x2 tooth plate

Faucet piece

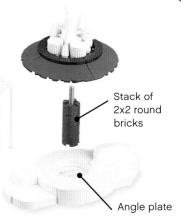

Bars, cones, and even tooth plates are used to make these microscale towers

A 2x2 brick at the base of this tower locks the four quarters of the main disk in place

Four 6x6 curved slopes attached to a 10x10 octagonal plate make up the main disk of the station

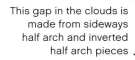

This gap in the clouds is made from sideways half arch and inverted half arch pieces

Stack of 2x2 round bricks

Angle plate

CLOUD BURST

The cloud-shaped base of this build is mostly built sideways. Cloud City itself fits on upright to an angle plate.

WHAT WILL YOU BUILD?
- Cloud-mining gear
- Seb's quarters
- Bespin globe

HUNT THE HUNTER

Seb races to the very top of Cloud City, where an observation tower is packed with tracking technology. He uses the equipment to scan the sky in all directions, and soon locates an unauthorized mining pod racing away from the station. He looks at his monitor screen and sees that the pod is holding Lando's barrel!

I'M GLAD I'M NOT SCARED OF HEIGHTS!

Antenna made from long bar

Small radar dish attaches to bar

2x2 dome

BOSSK IS BARRELING AWAY!

OBSERVATION TOWER

The observation tower is made almost entirely out of cylindrical parts—from long, thin bars to wide, flat round plates. Textured round bricks and small LEGO® Technic parts add machinelike detail.

Two 1x2 plates with end bar provide base for computer screen

4x4 round brick with holes adds texture to the side of the tower

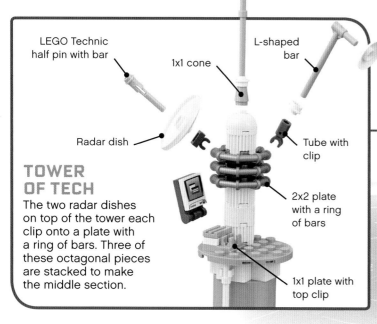

LEGO Technic half pin with bar

1x1 cone

L-shaped bar

Radar dish

Tube with clip

TOWER OF TECH

The two radar dishes on top of the tower each clip onto a plate with a ring of bars. Three of these octagonal pieces are stacked to make the middle section.

2x2 plate with a ring of bars

1x1 plate with top clip

1x2 brick with clip

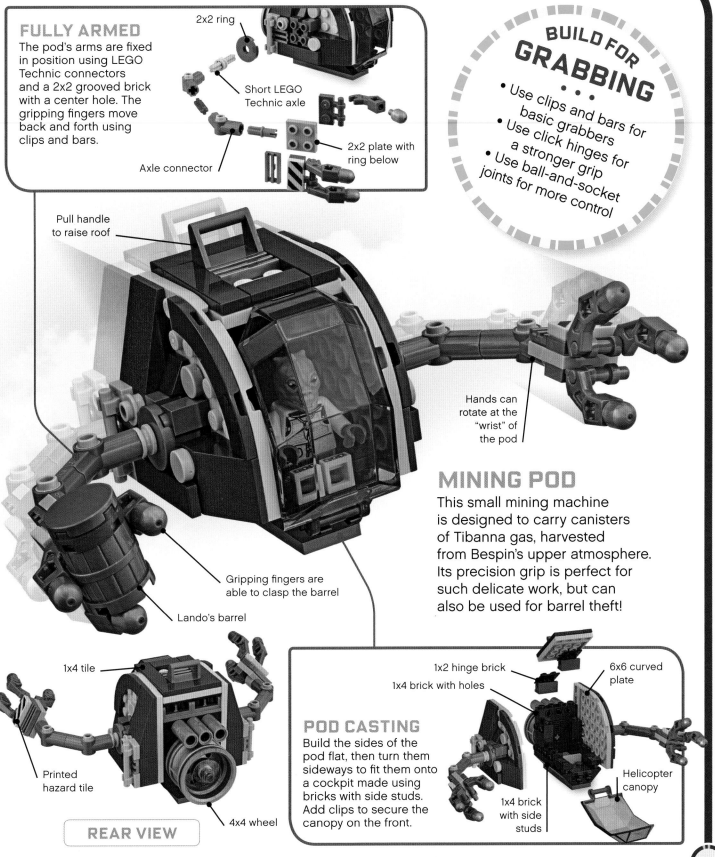

FULLY ARMED

The pod's arms are fixed in position using LEGO Technic connectors and a 2x2 grooved brick with a center hole. The gripping fingers move back and forth using clips and bars.

2x2 ring

Short LEGO Technic axle

Axle connector

2x2 plate with ring below

BUILD FOR GRABBING

• • •

- Use clips and bars for basic grabbers
- Use click hinges for a stronger grip
- Use ball-and-socket joints for more control

Pull handle to raise roof

Hands can rotate at the "wrist" of the pod

MINING POD

This small mining machine is designed to carry canisters of Tibanna gas, harvested from Bespin's upper atmosphere. Its precision grip is perfect for such delicate work, but can also be used for barrel theft!

Gripping fingers are able to clasp the barrel

Lando's barrel

1x4 tile

Printed hazard tile

4x4 wheel

REAR VIEW

1x2 hinge brick

1x4 brick with holes

6x6 curved plate

POD CASTING

Build the sides of the pod flat, then turn them sideways to fit them onto a cockpit made using bricks with side studs. Add clips to secure the canopy on the front.

1x4 brick with side studs

Helicopter canopy

START THE CAR!

There is no time to lose! Seb must chase Bossk before he gets away. He sends a message to the nearest docking bay and tells the droid on duty to get a cloud car ready for launch. When Seb reaches the bay, the droid is lifting the ship into position with a crane. Seb leaps into the pilot's seat and flies away!

SEB IS SO COOL ... FOR A HUMAN!

FUEL TANKS

The fuel tanks are astromech droid bodies with LEGO Technic parts where a droid's legs would usually go. Use the outer blue parts as connecting points for a fuel hose.

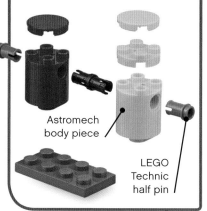

Astromech body piece

LEGO Technic half pin

DOCKING BAY SCENERY

You don't need lots of pieces to build a large docking bay. Several small builds, dotted around, give the sense of a much bigger space without the need to make every wall and surface.

TIME TO GET MY HEAD IN THE CLOUDS!

Maintenance ladder

CLOUD CAR PLATFORM

The base of this launch pad is a single 16x16 plate, but you could combine smaller plates to make yours. Similarly, if you don't have printed hazard tiles, make warning stripes from other bright pieces in your LEGO collection.

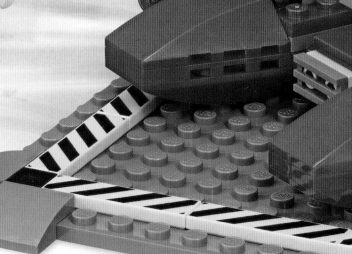

CRANE

As well as moving up and down, this crane arm can turn from side to side on a turntable plate. The base section is broad and solid so it doesn't tip over.

BUILD FOR STABILITY AND LIFTING

• Make the base of the crane heavier than the item you want to lift
• Test the strength of the crane as you build

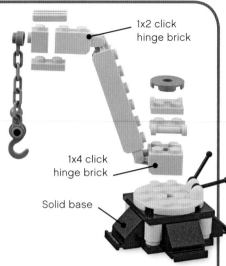

1x2 click hinge brick

1x4 click hinge brick

Solid base

IT ALL CLICKS

The crane arm is made from three click hinge bricks. These form a stronger connection than other hinge pieces, and will hold their position when lifting a reasonable load.

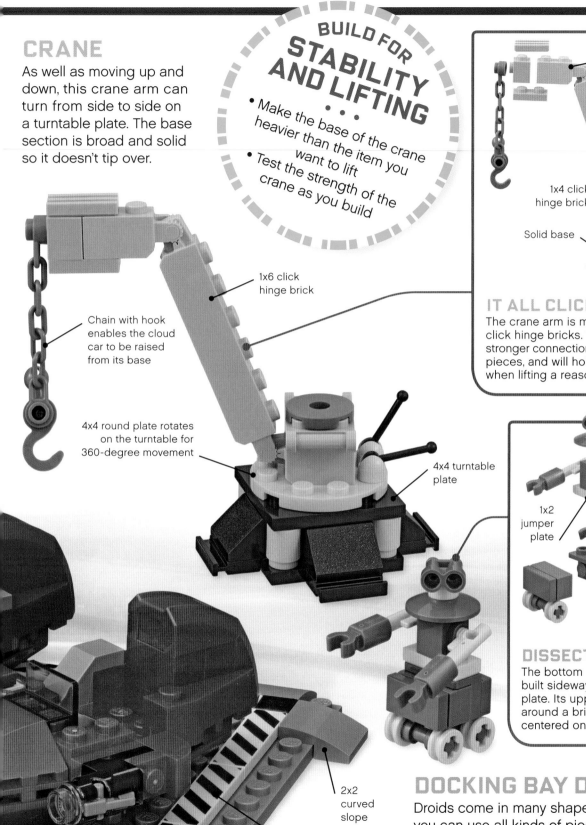

1x6 click hinge brick

Chain with hook enables the cloud car to be raised from its base

4x4 round plate rotates on the turntable for 360-degree movement

4x4 turntable plate

2x2 curved slope

1x4 printed hazard tile

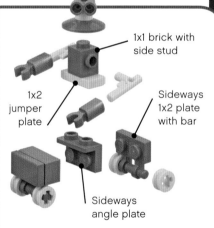

1x1 brick with side stud

1x2 jumper plate

Sideways 1x2 plate with bar

Sideways angle plate

DISSECTED DROID

The bottom half of the droid is built sideways using an angle plate. Its upper body is built around a brick with side studs, centered on a jumper plate.

DOCKING BAY DROID

Droids come in many shapes and sizes, and you can use all kinds of pieces to create your own designs. This one has binoculars for eyes and nozzle pieces for arms.

BOSSK'S BASE

Seb follows Bossk to a small asteroid closely orbiting Bespin. He lands his cloud car near the abandoned mining pod, where footprints lead into a cave. Inside, he finds a haul of valuables that Bossk has stolen, the assassin droid IG-88, and the bounty hunter himself ... magnetized by his armor to Lando's booby-trapped barrel!

WHAT A BARREL OF LAUGHS!

BASE ENTRANCE

The way into Bossk's cave base is through a blast-proof door. The use of colors and shapes in this build makes the back wall look like a metal door in rock.

1x3 inverted slope brick

1x1 slope on top of small cave wall

1x2 inverted slope brick

JUST HELPING MY FRIEND COUNT THE CASH!

1x1 round tiles serve as piles of coins

2x2 tile

2x2 jumper plate

ARGH! THIS IS A STICKY SITUATION!

COIN TABLE

This table looks like it has a completely smooth top. In fact, the piles of coins are built on the studs of a 2x3 plate, while the lone coin is attached to a jumper plate.

CAVE WALLS

Mixing different kinds of slopes in a range of similar colors is a great way to create realistic-looking rock walls. Gray pieces stand out as lights and pipes.

WHAT WILL YOU BUILD?
- Base defense droid
- Power generator
- Weapons rack

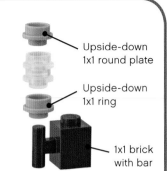

Upside-down 1x1 round plate

Upside-down 1x1 ring

1x1 brick with bar

TURN TO THE LIGHT

The cave lanterns are built onto a brick with a bar, starting with an upside-down 1x1 ring, followed by three upside-down 1x1 round plates.

1x3 slope brick

1x2 plate with bar

I'LL MAKE A MOVE WHILE HE CAN'T!

1x2 brick with pins makes for realistic pipework

CRATES

Bossk has stolen crates and barrels of different shapes and sizes and stashed them in his cave base. Each one is made with just a few pieces.

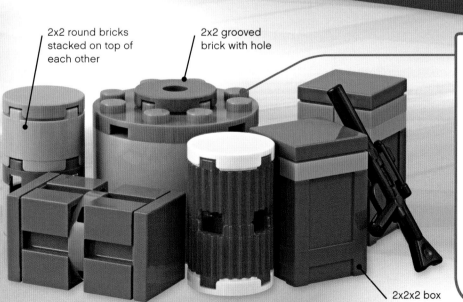

2x2 round bricks stacked on top of each other

2x2 grooved brick with hole

2x2x2 box

BARREL BUILD

The large barrel is built by attaching two curved bricks to a pair of round plates. Some of the other crates are made using stacked parts held together with axle pieces.

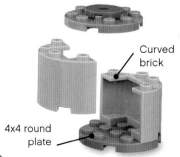

Curved brick

4x4 round plate

THE GREATEST CAPE

Unable to free himself, Bossk has no choice but to return to Cloud City with Seb. Lando meets them in his private quarters, using a secret code to demagnetize and open the barrel. Inside is a brand-new cape to add to his collection! Lando looks very happy, and very cool, as Bossk is marched to jail. Mission accomplished!

YOU'VE GOT ME OVER A BARREL!

BOT BREAKDOWN
The droid's wheels do not really turn, but they look realistic! They are made from LEGO Technic bushes on axle pins.

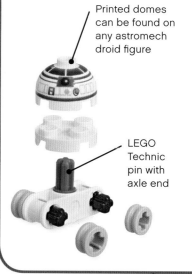

Printed domes can be found on any astromech droid figure

LEGO Technic pin with axle end

WHAT? NO CASH?

YOU CAN'T PUT A PRICE ON STYLE!

MY PRECIOUS CAPE!

Fabric minifigure cape

LEGO Technic bush

DOMESTIC DROID
Lando has a domestic droid in his quarters to keep everything neat and tidy. The droid is very happy to have a new cape to clean and press!

LANDO'S QUARTERS

The Baron Administrator of Cloud City likes his bedroom stylishly simple. It has plain walls, big windows, a large, comfy bed, and a walk-in closet with lots of room for clothes!

ON THE RAIL

Lando's cape rail is a short bar that slots into a brick with a side stud at one end. It doesn't touch the wall at the other end, so there is room to slide the capes on and off.

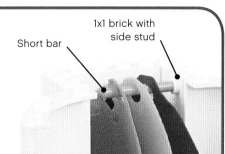

Short bar

1x1 brick with side stud

Two gray plates on top lock the wall sections in place

This large window is a transparent blue 1x6x5 wall piece

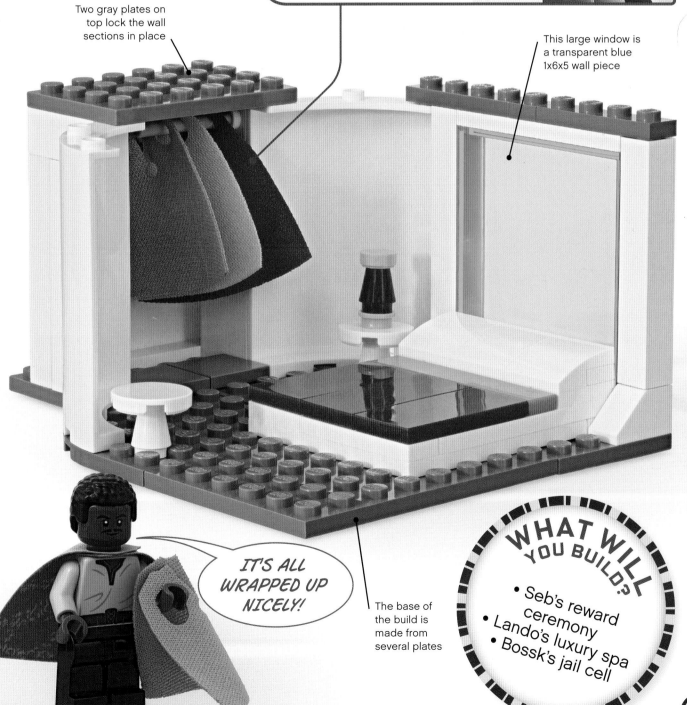

IT'S ALL WRAPPED UP NICELY!

The base of the build is made from several plates

WHAT WILL YOU BUILD?
• Seb's reward ceremony
• Lando's luxury spa
• Bossk's jail cell

CHAPTER 5
JAKKU

BACK TO JAKKU

When the Resistance hears that a new kind of TIE bomber has crashed on Jakku near the Star Destroyer, Rey says she will visit her old desert home to find it. There, her friend Finn sends her a holo-message. He tells Rey that they must learn the ship's secrets to defeat the First Order. But she must reach it before the stormtroopers!

COME IN, REY! COME IN, REY!

Long antenna piece

1x1 round plate

1x2 printed tile

1x1 round brick

BASE TO FINN

A simple receiver should have chunky power cells (in this case, round bricks), a control panel (here, a printed tile), an antenna, and a projector lens (a simple 1x1 round tile).

BRIEFING POST

Rey knows that when she gets to Jakku she will be able to build a holographic receiver from all the space junk on the planet. You can use any LEGO® pieces to build one of your own!

Antenna slots into 2x2 round brick

LOOK OUT FOR THIS WRECK. THE TIE BOMBER'S NEARBY!

A 1x1 brick with bar makes a carry handle for the receiver unit

Just two tan-colored plates can suggest a sandy desert surface

THANKS FINN. I'LL CHECK THE WRECKS!

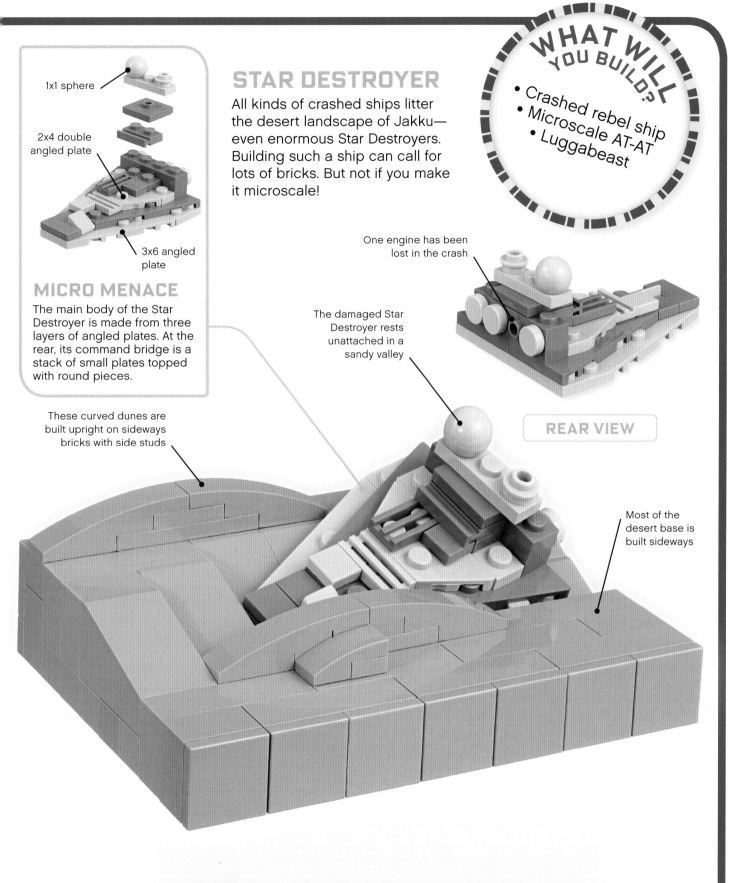

STAR DESTROYER

All kinds of crashed ships litter the desert landscape of Jakku—even enormous Star Destroyers. Building such a ship can call for lots of bricks. But not if you make it microscale!

1x1 sphere

2x4 double angled plate

3x6 angled plate

WHAT WILL YOU BUILD?
- Crashed rebel ship
- Microscale AT-AT
- Luggabeast

MICRO MENACE

The main body of the Star Destroyer is made from three layers of angled plates. At the rear, its command bridge is a stack of small plates topped with round pieces.

One engine has been lost in the crash

The damaged Star Destroyer rests unattached in a sandy valley

REAR VIEW

These curved dunes are built upright on sideways bricks with side studs

Most of the desert base is built sideways

MEET THE OLD BOSS

Flying straight to the wreckage would alert the First Order to Rey's presence on Jakku, so she starts her mission at Niima Outpost, the planet's busy market. She tracks down her old boss, trader Unkar Plutt, and asks him for transport into the desert. He offers her use of his broken landspeeder, if she can make it work!

HAVEN'T I SEEN YOU BEFORE?

USE YOUR HEAD
The water bottles hanging from the stall are made from transparent blue minifigure head pieces with no face printing.

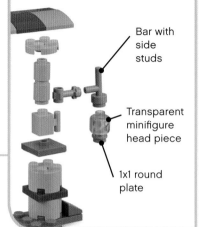

Bar with side studs

Transparent minifigure head piece

1x1 round plate

LEGO® Technic steering wheel

WATER TRADER
Don't expect to drink for free on Jakku! This trader controls the watering hole and will accept salvaged valuables in exchange for a thirst-quenching cup or bottle of water.

2x2 jumper plates enable bottles and cups to be attached to the table top

2x2 inverted slope brick

WATER WAY TO MAKE A LIVING!

WATERING HOLE
Water is precious on a desert world. This well is one of the most important places on Jakku! Loose transparent 1x1 round plates are used to make the water.

Walls of the well made from 4x4 curved bricks

62

PLUTT'S STALL

Unkar Plutt is a ruthless trader with a hand in all that happens on Jakku. Rey is wary of him, but she knows his stall is the place to go for spare parts—or even a whole vehicle.

Tube with clip

1x2 plate with top clip

2x2 curved slope

1x4 tile

STALL AWNING

The awning over Plutt's stall is made from curved slopes and smooth tiles built on a 4x10 plate. The awning over the water trader's stall is built the same way on a 2x10 plate.

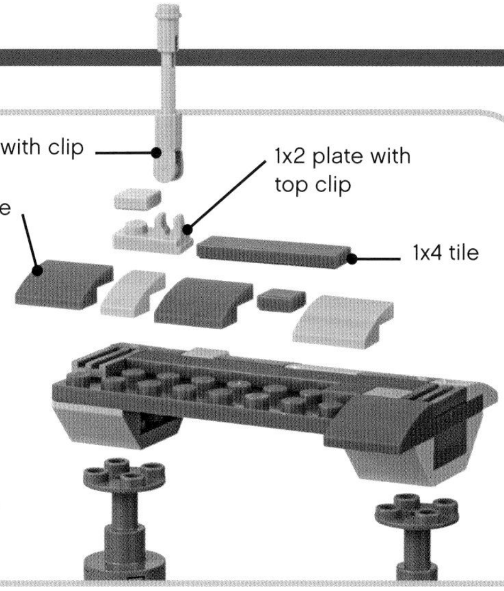

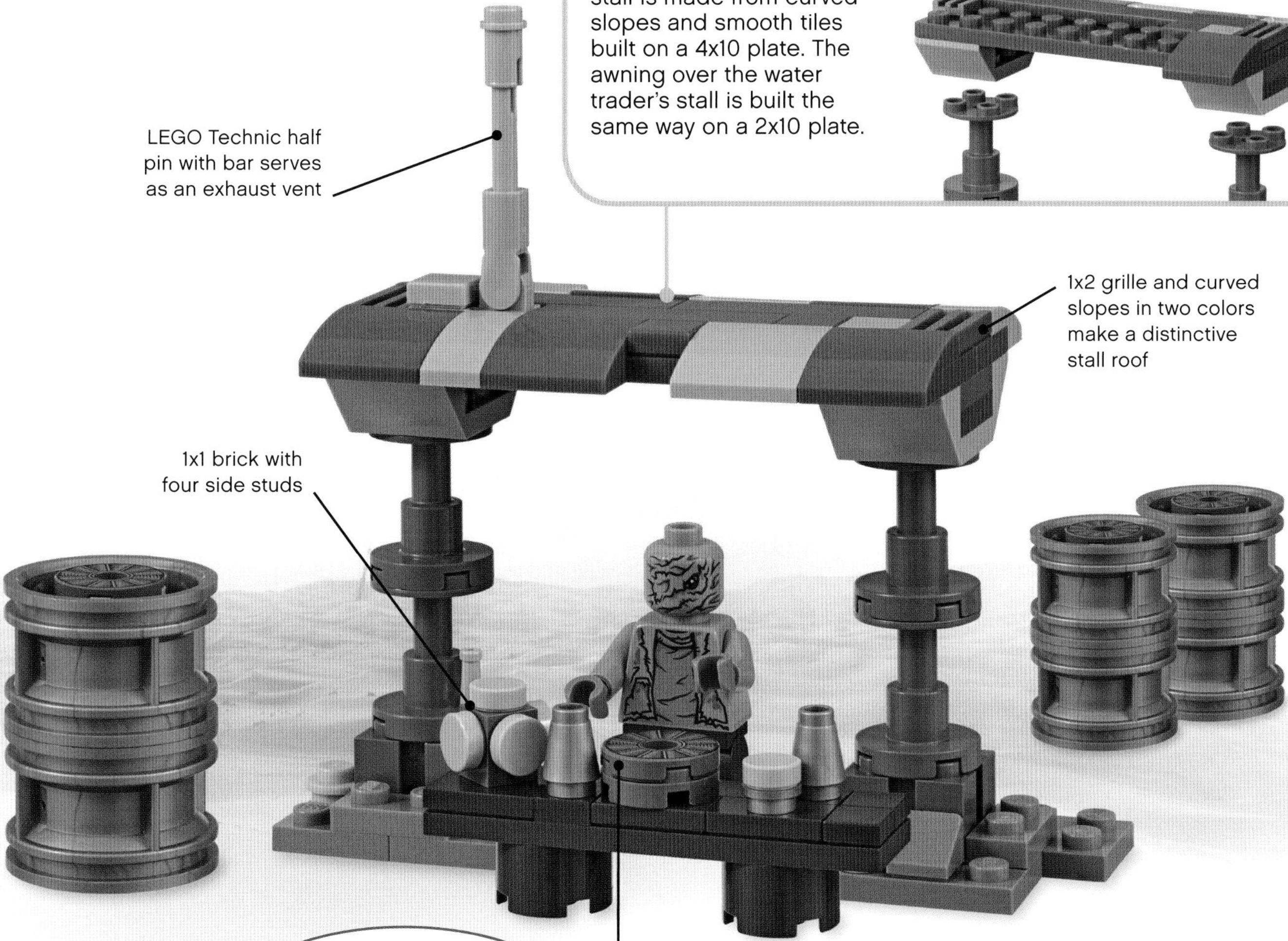

LEGO Technic half pin with bar serves as an exhaust vent

1x2 grille and curved slopes in two colors make a distinctive stall roof

1x1 brick with four side studs

LEGO Technic wheels make good starship engines

HAVE YOU SEEN A TIE ANYWHERE?

I NEVER WEAR A SUIT!

WHAT WILL YOU BUILD?

- Rey's Resistance ship
- Outpost gateway
- Plutt's junkyard

DESERT DASH

Rey soon gets the landspeeder to work, and flies off into the desert to search for the TIE. Up ahead, she sees a First Order transport, already on its way to the crash site. She pushes the landspeeder to its limits to overtake it, and dodges blaster fire from the stormtroopers on board as she races ahead!

SHE'S FAST, BUT WE'RE ... OH.

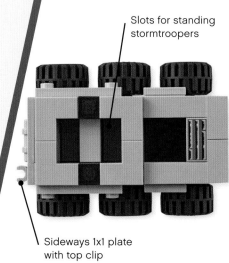

Slots for standing stormtroopers

Sideways 1x1 plate with top clip

OTHER VIEW

1x1 transluscent red round brick is an effective warning light

THEY SHOULD CALL US THE FAST ORDER!

Long bar

First Order officer in the driver's seat

Printed 1x2 tile

Chunky tires help to travel over the desert terrain

FIRST ORDER TRANSPORT

There is space for two troopers to stand in the back of this vehicle, while a driver sits in front. It has six wheels to spread its weight across the soft desert sand.

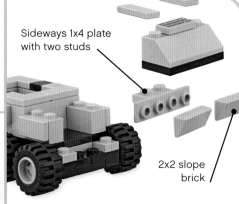

Sideways 1x4 plate with two studs

2x2 slope brick

SMOOTH AND CHUNKY

Sideways plates and tiles give this vehicle its chunky, armored look. The tiles on top and the slopes at the front add to its smooth, streamlined finish.

Bricks and slopes create a desert backdrop

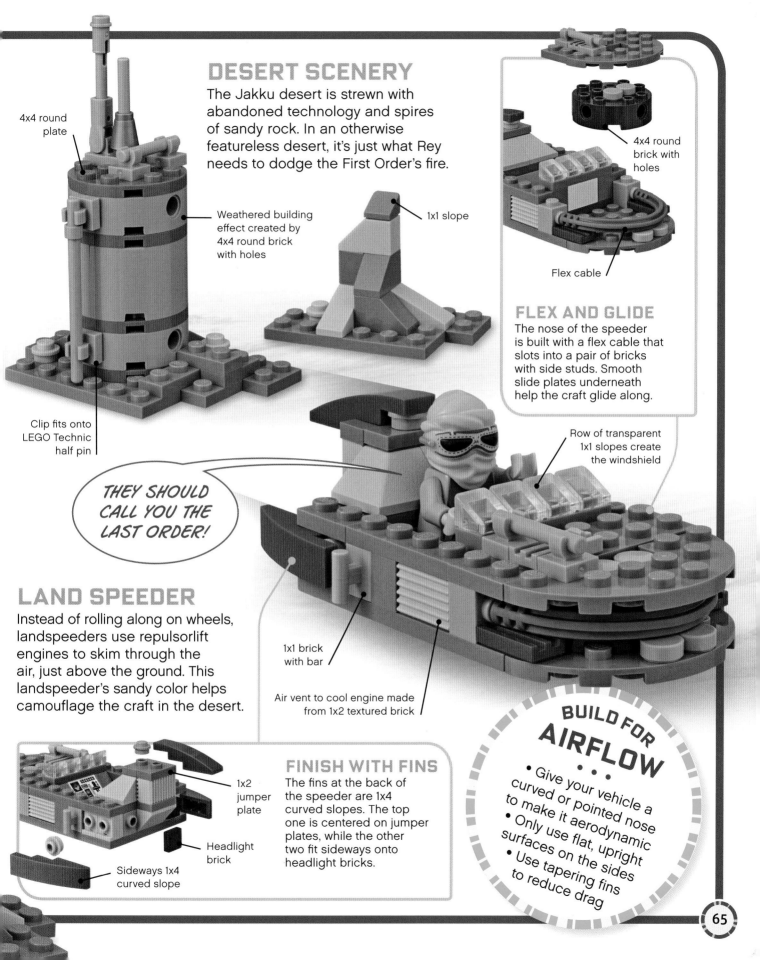

DESERT SCENERY

The Jakku desert is strewn with abandoned technology and spires of sandy rock. In an otherwise featureless desert, it's just what Rey needs to dodge the First Order's fire.

4x4 round plate

Weathered building effect created by 4x4 round brick with holes

1x1 slope

4x4 round brick with holes

Flex cable

FLEX AND GLIDE

The nose of the speeder is built with a flex cable that slots into a pair of bricks with side studs. Smooth slide plates underneath help the craft glide along.

Clip fits onto LEGO Technic half pin

Row of transparent 1x1 slopes create the windshield

THEY SHOULD CALL YOU THE LAST ORDER!

LAND SPEEDER

Instead of rolling along on wheels, landspeeders use repulsorlift engines to skim through the air, just above the ground. This landspeeder's sandy color helps camouflage the craft in the desert.

1x1 brick with bar

Air vent to cool engine made from 1x2 textured brick

FINISH WITH FINS

The fins at the back of the speeder are 1x4 curved slopes. The top one is centered on jumper plates, while the other two fit sideways onto headlight bricks.

1x2 jumper plate

Headlight brick

Sideways 1x4 curved slope

BUILD FOR AIRFLOW
· · ·
• Give your vehicle a curved or pointed nose to make it aerodynamic
• Only use flat, upright surfaces on the sides
• Use tapering fins to reduce drag

REY IN THE RUINS

At top speed, it doesn't take Rey long to reach the rusting desert wreck that she used to call home. Inside, she finds the place just as she left it—full of salvaged gadgets and half-built machines. This is just what she needs to recover the TIE bomber and see off the stormtroopers. She knows they won't be far behind!

I HAVEN'T MISSED THIS PLACE!

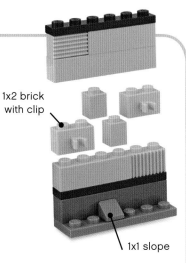

1x2 brick with clip

1x1 slope

CLIP TIP
Build bricks or plates with clips into your walls so they can hold tools and other equipment.

WORKSHOP
Most of Rey's old home is given over to her workshop, where she once spent her days repairing the tech she salvaged from the desert. Just a few parts are needed to make its rusty metal walls.

1x2 textured brick

Oilcan attaches to wall by sideways 1x1 top clip

Wrench

I KNOW JUST WHAT I NEED TO BUILD!

Spanner

Surface of workbench made up of 1x1 plates and 1x2 jumper plates

WORKBENCHES
Though the items look randomly scattered on Rey's two workbenches, each one is held in place with a stud or a clip precisely for that purpose.

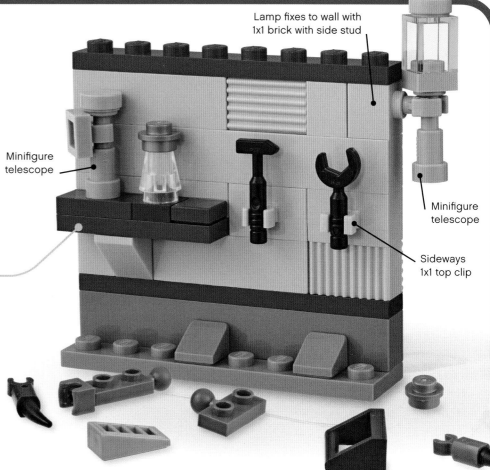

Lamp fixes to wall with
1x1 brick with side stud

Minifigure
telescope

Minifigure
telescope

Sideways
1x1 top clip

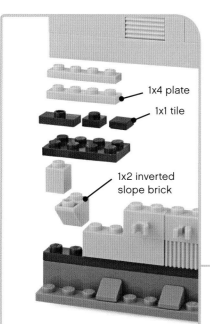

1x4 plate

1x1 tile

1x2 inverted
slope brick

SHELF STACKING
The shelf in the workshop wall is
a 2x4 plate, firmly sandwiched
between bricks above and
below it. It is topped with a tile,
a plate, and a jumper plate.

L-shaped bar

LEGO Technic gear

LEGO Technic
axle with stud end

Sideways
headlight brick

1x1 plate
with top clip

1x2
inverted
slope

PARTS PILE
You can grab pretty much any
handful of LEGO pieces to make
an interesting spare parts pile.
Some of these parts are built onto
the base, while others are loose.

WHAT WILL
YOU BUILD?

• Secret water stash
• Rey's hammock
• Rey's stove

TIE RESCUE

Working faster than ever before, Rey uses all her skills to build a crane that can lift the crashed TIE bomber out of the sand. And if any troopers get too close, she can also grab them with its claw! The First Order can only watch as she frees the top-secret fighter and flies it away to safety. Mission well and truly accomplished!

SHE NEEDS TO GO ON A CRASH COURSE!

SHE'S ONE FAST ENGINEER!

CRASH SITE

This experimental TIE bomber not only has a cockpit and solar collector panels like an ordinary TIE fighter, but also a large bomb bay. One of its solar collectors has broken off in the crash that stranded the bomber on Jakku.

2x8 plate

Bomb bay

Cockpit accommodates one pilot—this one was unlucky enough to crash

Broken solar collector

2x4 double-angled plate

Transparent red printed radar dish

WHOLE MODEL

1x4 spring-shooter brick

Sideways jet engine piece

1x2/1x4 upward angle plate

TWIN ENGINES

The main body of the TIE bomber is made from two large jet engine pieces. These are built sideways around a spring-shooter brick using two different types of angle plate.

68

BUILD FOR FLEXIBILITY

- Use ball-and-socket joints for 360-degree movement
- Use hinge joints for up and down movement
- Add extra joints for snake-like movement

1x2 plate with rail

SCAVENGER CRANE

Rey's homemade crane has four adjustable legs for stability on uneven surfaces, and a crane arm with six poseable joints. It is made from gray and brown pieces to suggest rusty metal.

1x2 plate with handled bar

REAR VIEW

TIME FOR SOME STRONG-ARM TACTICS!

Joystick pieces used for the crane's control levers

1x4 plate with tubes

Sideways 1x2 handle

Horn pieces for grabbing objects

1x2 ball-and-socket plate gives the crane flexibility when crossing rocky terrain

1x2 ball plate

CRANE ARM

The crane has three ball-and-socket joints along its arm, and three clip-and-bar hinge joints making up its grabber. The precision grabber tips are made from horn pieces.

1x2 ball plate

1x2 ball-and-socket plate

1x2 plate with handled bar

Tube with clip

Horn piece

CLOUD CITY CAR

Seb and his fellow members of the Bespin
Wing Guard patrol the skies around Cloud City in
Storm IV Twin-Pod cloud cars. Each car has room
for two guards, or for a single guard and a prisoner.
Seb's cloud car is powered by a repulsorlift engine
between its two pods, and has small but powerful
blaster cannons on either side.

I LOVE A
SKY-HIGH
MISSION!

Transparisteel
windshield is
blaster-proof

Gunner's seat
or prisoner pod

Combined
repulsorlift and
ion engine unit

Blaster cannons are
working stud shooters

BUILDING INSTRUCTIONS

1

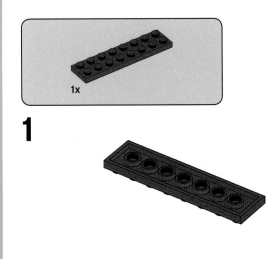

1x

2

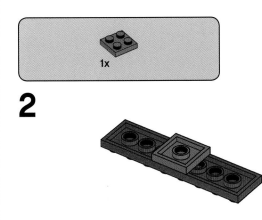

1x

3

2x

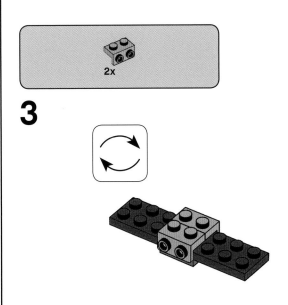

BEEP

4

1x

5

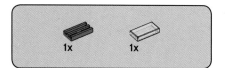

1x   1x

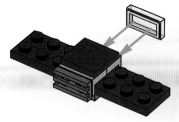

6

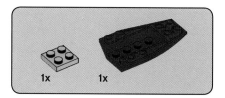

1x   1x

7

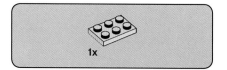

1x

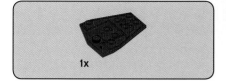

8

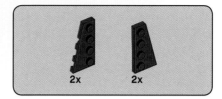

10

2x

9

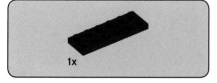

11

12

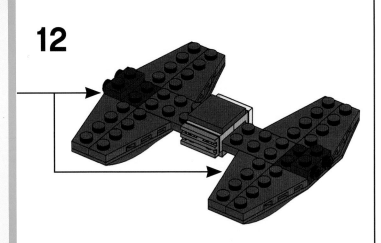

13

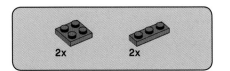

2x 2x

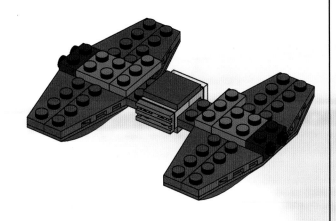

14

4x

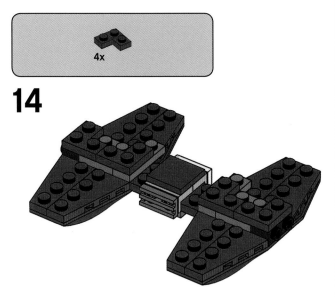

15

2x 2x

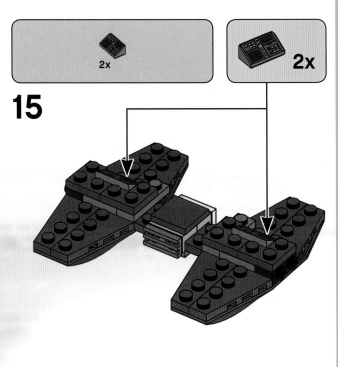

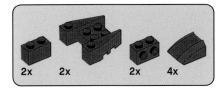

16

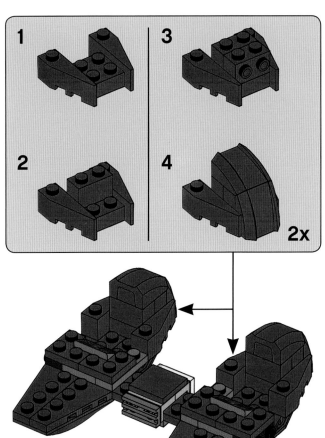

17

> I'M TRACKING DOWN THE BAD GUYS!

18

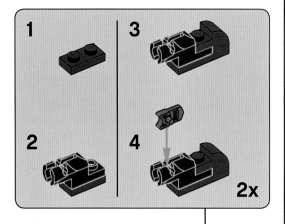

1

2

3

4

2x

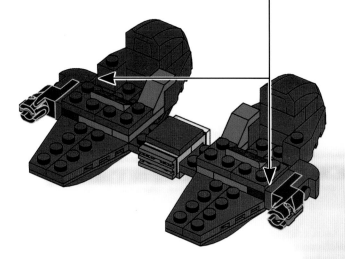

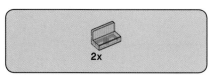

19

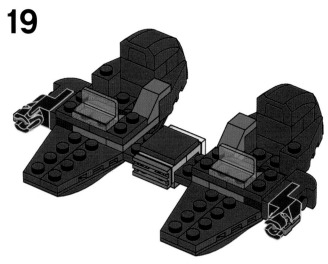

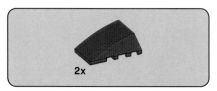

20

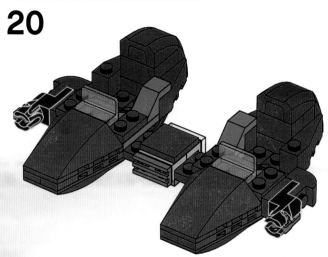

21

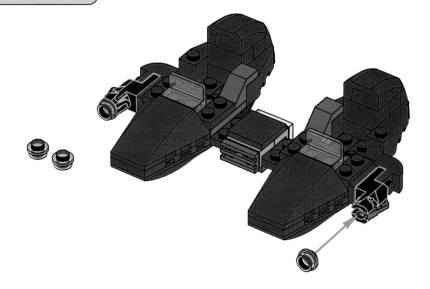

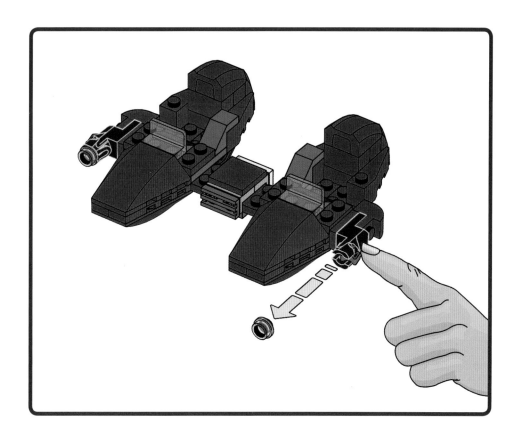

4x

Penguin
Random
House

Senior Editors Phil Hunt, Victoria Taylor
Senior Designer Anna Formanek
Assistant Designer James McKeag
Pre-Production Producer Siu Yin Chan
Senior Producer Louise Daly
Managing Editor Paula Regan
Managing Art Editor Jo Connor
Publisher Julie Ferris
Art Director Lisa Lanzarini
Publishing Director Simon Beecroft

Written by Simon Hugo
Inspirational models built by Rod Gillies
Photography by Gary Ombler

Dorling Kindersley would like to thank Randi Sørensen,
Heidi K. Jensen, Paul Hansford, Martin Leighton Lindhardt,
Henrik Andersen and Torben Vad Nissen at the LEGO Group,
as well as Jennifer Heddle, Michael Siglain, Leland Chee,
Derek Stothard, Julia Vargas, Stephanie Everett, and
Chelsea Alon at Lucasfilm. Thanks also to Beth Davies
and Julia March for editorial assistance, and
Megan Douglass at DK for proofreading.

First American Edition, 2019
Published in the United States by DK Publishing
1450 Broadway, Suite 801, New York, New York 10018

Page design copyright © 2019 Dorling Kindersley Limited
DK, a Division of Penguin Random House LLC
18 19 20 21 22 10 9 8 7 6 5 4 3 2 1
001–311505–Aug/2019

LEGO, the LEGO logo, the Minifigure, and the Brick and Knob
configurations are trademarks and/or copyrights of the LEGO Group.
All rights reserved. ©2019 The LEGO Group.
Manufactured by Dorling Kindersley, 80 Strand, London,
WC2R 0RL, UK, under license from the LEGO Group.

© & TM 2019 LUCASFILM LTD

All rights reserved. Without limiting the rights under the
copyright reserved above, no part of this publication may
be reproduced, stored in or introduced into a retrieval
system, or transmitted, in any form, or by any means
(electronic, mechanical, photocopying, recording,
or otherwise), without the prior written permission
of the copyright owner.

Published in Great Britain by Dorling Kindersley Limited

A catalog record for this book
is available from the Library of Congress.
ISBN 978-1-4654-7895-5

DK books are available at special discounts when
purchased in bulk for sales promotions, premiums,
fund-raising, or educational use. For details, contact:
DK Publishing Special Markets,
1450 Broadway, Suite 801, New York, New York 10018
SpecialSales@dk.com

Printed in China

www.LEGO.com
www.dk.com

A WORLD OF IDEAS:
SEE ALL THERE IS TO KNOW

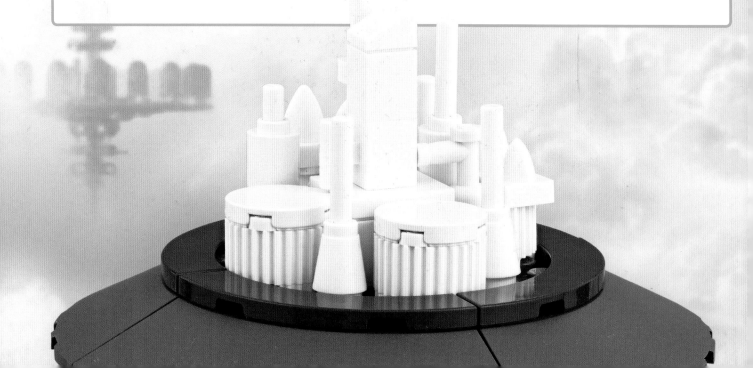